Treasury of Illustrated Classics™

Gulliver's Travels

by
Jonathan Swift

Adapted by
D. J. Arneson

Illustrated by
Eva Clift

Modern Publishing
A Division of Unisystems, Inc.
New York, New York 10022

Series UPC: 39340

Cover art by Ned Butterfield

Copyright ©1998, 2002, 2003 Kidsbooks, Inc.
230 Fifth Avenue
New York, New York 10001

This edition published by Modern Publishing,
a division of Unisystems, Inc.

Printed in Italy

Contents

Chapter 1

A Voyage to
Lilliput

"There it is!" I shouted. "The carriage for London."

Four powerful black horses pulling a dust-covered carriage appeared on the road leading to my father's small estate. The carriage swayed like a ship on a stormy sea. In a few minutes, I would say good-bye to my father and begin a life of adventure.

The carriage stopped, and I climbed in. I stuck my head out the window. "I want to see the whole wide world, Father," I said.

My father smiled. "Lemuel," he said, "you're only fourteen years old. You can travel wherever you want, but first you have to finish school. The time will pass faster than you think."

The driver cracked his whip, and the carriage lurched. I waved a last good-bye. I was on my way.

My years in London passed quickly, just as my father said. I became a doctor's apprentice, and later, I went to Holland to study medicine. I also learned sailing and navigation because I knew they would be useful on long voyages.

I became a ship's surgeon and went to sea. I traveled far and wide for six years and learned the customs and languages of many people. Then, in 1699, the captain of the *Antelope* offered me a position on his ship. I accepted. We set sail from Bristol on May fourth.

We were well on our way to the East Indies when a violent storm struck our ship. Its fierce winds tossed us over the foaming waves and blew us far off course. We had no idea where we were.

When the seas calmed down, we found ourselves in a desperate situation. We were somewhere northwest of the island of Tasmania. Twelve of our crew were dead and the rest were dangerously weak. I was tending to the sick when I heard a shout.

"Captain," the lookout screamed. "We're going to crash!"

I looked up in time to see a huge black rock jutting from the sea, directly

in our path. The ship heeled violently as the steersman spun the wheel to avoid a collision. It was too late. We crashed headlong into the rock. The ship split in half like a stick cracked across a knee.

"Abandon ship!" the captain shouted as giant waves rushed over the torn hull. I was swept from the deck and thrown into the roiling sea. My world turned a

deep, dark green as I was dragged under the water. I clawed at the water as if I were climbing an invisible ladder until, at last, I bobbed to the surface. The bow of the *Antelope* loomed over my head. The ship lurched, and with a rush of air that sounded like a sigh, the proud ship slipped under the waves and was gone.

"Mr. Gulliver! Mr. Gulliver! Over here!" said the first mate. He and four others clung to the side of a boat that skimmed down the slope of a towering wave toward me. I grabbed his hand as the boat shot by. Once we were clear of the rock, I clambered aboard. We were saved, but we were at the mercy of the pounding sea.

"To the oars men!" the mate shouted. "Pull for your lives!"

We each grabbed an oar and began to row. It was all we could do to keep the bow pointed into the raging wind. It was hopeless. One by one, the men fell over their oars, exhausted. The boat drifted helplessly. A hissing sound filled the air, louder than the roar of the storm. The sky turned blacker than black as a rogue wave taller than a ship's mast loomed over the horizon. It headed for our small boat with the speed of a cannonball. It struck us broadside and lifted us into the air. We hung in space for a second and then fell back into the sea, upside down. When I came to the surface this time, the sea was empty. The boat was gone and my companions had disappeared. I never saw them again.

The raging wind and tide pushed me across the water like a cork. I swam for my life, but it was hopeless. I knew the next wave would claim me and I would join my shipmates. I stopped swimming, ready to give up the struggle. My feet struck something solid. It was the bottom! I could stand! "I am saved!" I shouted over the wind.

My will to survive returned. I wiped the wind-blown foam from my face and turned a full circle, seeking a glimpse of land. There was no beach in sight. I was determined not to perish, so I turned my back to the wind and began walking through the waist-deep water.

I had walked about a mile when I spied an empty beach through the mists of the dying storm. I hurried toward it and did not stop until my feet were firmly planted on the exposed sand. The beach was as empty as a farmer's field in winter. "Is this my fate?" I asked aloud. "I am alive, but how long can I survive in a barren place like this?"

I pushed inland, hoping to find signs of life, but the land was as bare as the beach. By nightfall, I was too tired to take another step. I found a patch of grass and lay down on my back, exhausted. I closed my eyes and fell into a deep sleep. I had never slept more soundly.

Chapter 2

I Am Captured!

The sun was high in the sky when I awoke. I blinked my eyes. The memory of the storm and my comrades' fate seemed like a bad dream. I remembered where I was and I smiled. "I am safe," I said. "That is all that matters."

No sooner were the words out of my mouth than I heard a faint rustling sound, like the scurrying of small animals in the grass. I thought nothing of it. My first task was to explore this place and find help.

I tried to lift my head, but it wouldn't move. "What's this?" I said. "Have I tangled my hair in brambles?" I tried to raise my arms to feel my hair, but I couldn't move them, either. I tried lifting my legs, but they were also stuck to the ground. I was thoroughly puzzled.

I tipped my head forward an inch and turned my eyes down as far as they would go. "Great heavens!" I exclaimed. "I am tied to the ground!" I couldn't believe my eyes. My entire body was covered by hundreds of tiny ropes no thicker than a thread. They were everywhere, crossing my chest, arms, and legs as if a giant spider had woven me into its web. Each rope was tied to a pin-sized stake that was driven solidly into the ground. My long hair was also tied to stakes. I lay on my back in the hot sun, unable to move. I was dumbfounded. "I am a prisoner!" I cried. "But who has captured me?"

I heard the rustling sound again. At the same time, something moved up my left leg. I thought a mouse had found me. I wanted to bat it away, but my arm wouldn't budge.

The creature walked over my stomach and moved slowly to my chest, where it stopped just below my chin. I took a huge gulp of air, thinking I could blow it away. But when I tipped my eyes again to see what it was, the air rushed out in a gasp. "Whooof!" I exclaimed. "This is not possible!"

Standing in the middle of my chest, staring into my face as if I had just fallen from the sky, was a perfectly formed little

man less than six inches tall! I blinked twenty times in disbelief, but each time my eyes opened, he was still there. He wore ordinary clothes and looked every bit like anyone I had ever seen in London. In his hands was a miniature bow loaded with a tiny arrow smaller than a sewing needle. A quiver filled with more arrows was slung on his back. "A little man!" I exclaimed.

At the sound of my voice, the man raised his bow and pointed it at my nose. At the same time, another ripple of tiny footsteps scampered up my body and no fewer than forty more little men formed a rank behind the first. "I am dreaming!" I shouted as loud as I could, hoping the noise would wake me up. Instead, it rolled like thunder and the little people ran for their lives, jumping and falling to the ground.

The place was silent for many long minutes. Then a murmur rose from the grass. As curiosity got the best of them, the band of little men cautiously climbed back onto my chest. The first man I had seen was the leader and was bolder than the others. He walked close to my chin and tapped it with the tip of his bow. He peered into my face and opened his mouth to speak. He had to shout for me to hear his shrill little voice, but his language was one I had never heard. "I can't understand you," I whispered so I wouldn't frighten him.

I wanted to face him so I struggled to break my bonds. I pulled my left arm free and turned my head slightly. The moment I moved, a shout went up and the little men scattered like a swarm of bees. They immediately regrouped on top of my stomach. At a command from their leader, they shot a shower of tiny arrows at me. The arrows stung my raised hand like needles. Some arrows struck my body and bounced off, but a flight of them flew into my face. "Ouch!" I cried as I put up my hand to protect my eyes.

The more I struggled, the more arrows hit me. They were joined by a series of lance thrusts that pierced my coat. I knew it would be wiser to lie still. "Stop," I said. "I give up." The moment I stopped moving, the arrows stopped. I put my head back, relieved that the stinging attack was over.

Soon the air was filled with the noise of hammering and sawing. It mixed with the rustling and murmuring of the crowd of tiny people gathered around me. I turned my head to see what they were doing. A band of miniature carpenters was hard at work constructing a stage next to my head. When it was finished, an important-looking man attended by three servants no taller than my index finger climbed a ladder to the platform at its top. He looked down into my face and began to talk. He made a long speech that I could not understand, but I judged by the tone of his voice that he was asking me to behave.

"Oh, yes," I said in a tone that he would understand. The man shouted an order to the people below and the ropes holding me down were cut.

The man spoke again in words that sounded like promises, threats, pity, and kindness. He paused for my reply. "I am at your mercy," I said with a smile so he would not mistake my intention.

The man nodded.

"I am very hungry," I said, putting my hand to my mouth as if eating.

The great lord shouted to the throng below. In moments, dozens of ladders were placed against my sides and a hundred tiny people carrying baskets filled with food scrambled up them. I learned later that the food was sent by the emperor.

I ate heartily. The meat was the whole shoulders and legs of animals, but to me they were as small as birds' wings. I ate two or three at a time. The bread loaves were no bigger than fat peas, and I ate those by the mouthful. I made a sign that I was thirsty and two large barrels were rolled to me. Each one held about a half pint. I easily emptied them in two swallows. When I finished my meal, I put my hand to my lips to cover a polite burp.

The crowd roared with approval, and those on my chest danced for joy. I was tempted to grab a handful of them, but I had promised not to escape. I was bound by the laws of hospitality they showed me.

A short time later, a high-ranking person strolled across my chest and stopped a few inches in front of my face. He held up a scroll with the royal sign on it to show that he had been sent by the emperor. "I recognize a royal seal when I see one," I said, nodding to be sure he knew I understood. He turned to the horizon and pointed with a gesture that made it clear I would be taken there.

"But first you must cut the rest of my bonds," I said, making a sawing sign with my fingers. The man shook his head firmly. "I see," I said sadly, "I am still your prisoner." I thought of breaking free, but the memory of the stinging arrows and the blisters they raised changed my mind. My eyes began to flutter, and I drifted into a deep slumber. I was told later that my drink was drugged and I heard about what happened while I slept.

The emperor had ordered five hundred carpenters to build a machine large enough to carry me to the capital. It was a long wooden platform on twenty-two wheels. Strong ropes were tied to my body and slung over pulleys on top of foot-high poles. Nine hundred of their strongest men lifted me off the ground and lowered me onto the platform, where I was tied down, still sleeping. Fifteen hundred tiny horses only four-and-a-half inches tall pulled the platform to the capital. The journey took a day and a half. I didn't wake until a curious guard poked his spear up my nose.

"Aaaachoo!" I sneezed, and the blast blew the poor fellow into the air like a feather. I glanced around. We had stopped next to an ancient temple just outside the city gates. The temple was the largest in the kingdom, and even it was no larger than a dining-room table. It was determined I should live here. The emperor was already coming toward me on horseback.

After dismounting, the emperor ordered a crew of blacksmiths to attach dozens of tiny chains to my right leg and lock them to the front of the temple. The chains were long enough for me to walk a few steps or to crawl into the temple, which would be my new home. Unfortunately, they were also strong enough to hold me.

Other workers cut the bonds holding me to the platform and I immediately stood up and stretched. The crowd gasped as my shadow covered thousands of them like a dark blanket.

I placed my hands on my hips and surveyed the miniature kingdom spread out before me. The country was as tidy as an English garden. Corn fields looked like flower beds, and forests stood no higher than hedges. The tallest trees were only seven feet high. The nearby city reminded me of a toy village. It was barely large enough to fill an average town square.

The emperor came toward me. He put his hand to his chin and walked around me just beyond the reach of my chain. He studied me up and down. When he was satisfied that I was his prisoner, he ordered his chefs to bring me a feast.

The emperor was joined by the empress, a number of princes and princesses, and their attendants. Everyone watched in awe as, with gusto, I emptied twenty carts filled with food and drink.

The emperor was a handsome fellow, a little over six inches tall. His clothes were rather plain, but the glittering gold, jewel-encrusted crown on his head left no doubt about his rank. His right hand held a shining, three-inch sword. There was no doubt he would use it if I broke loose. I held back a smile so he would not be offended.

"You have a beautiful kingdom, Your Excellency," I said in a tone of admiration.

The emperor turned his face up to mine and spoke in a shrill voice. I took his reply to mean, "Thank you."

After a time, the emperor and his court returned to the capital. I remained behind, chained to the temple wall.

A strong troop of the emperor's guards surrounded my feet. Behind

them, pushing and shoving for a closer look, was a vast crowd of tiny people. I was as interested in them as they were in me, and for a long time we exchanged silent gazes. As I turned to the opposite side, a group of troublemakers began shooting arrows at me. One arrow struck close to my eye. The colonel of the guard saw what had happened. He ordered his men to seize the culprits and tie them up. He delivered them to me for punishment.

I leaned down and scooped up all six in one hand. "Now let us see how brave you are," I said. Their faces went blank with horror. They did not understand my words, but my intention was clear. I lifted them high over my head. The terrified men squawked like a nest of chirping birds. I popped five of them into my breast pocket, but kept one tightly clenched in my fist.

I opened my mouth as wide as I could and held him in front of it so that to him, the view would be straight down my throat. He squirmed and screamed as I took my penknife from my pocket and placed its point on his chest. I smacked my lips as if I were going to eat him. "What a tender morsel," I said.

The colonel paced nervously at my feet. He winced when he saw my shiny blade move against the man's chest. With a motion as quick as a toad hop, I cut the man's bonds and lowered him gently to the ground. I took the others from my pocket and set them next to the first man. "You didn't think I would harm you, did you?" I said with a laugh. The colonel breathed a deep sigh of relief as the troublemakers turned on their heels and disappeared in a cloud of dust. The crowd roared its approval at my kindness. The colonel was very pleased.

Chapter 3

I Ask for Freedom

When night fell, I crawled into my new home to rest. I had to sleep on the ground because there wasn't anything in the kingdom large enough for me to lie on. Later, the emperor ordered his workers to make a bed for me. They carted six hundred mattresses into my little house and sewed them together four deep. An army of seamstresses sewed hundreds of sheets and blankets together to make bed covers.

Word of my arrival in the tiny kingdom quickly spread across the land. Every morning an immense crowd waited outside my house to see me. I was such a curiosity that farmers abandoned their fields and women left their work to come and stare. It got so bad that the emperor ordered everyone to go back home. Nobody was permitted to return unless they bought a license.

Meanwhile, the emperor and his counselors met to decide my fate. They worried that if I escaped, my huge appetite would cause a famine. At first, they thought to starve me or shoot me in the face with poisoned arrows. Then the emperor heard I had let the six troublemakers go free. He and his court were so impressed that he immediately ordered that I should be properly fed and cared for.

Every morning after that, six cattle, forty sheep, and large quantities of bread and other food were delivered to my house. Six hundred servants were assigned to look after me and three hundred tailors were ordered to sew new clothes. My greatest joy was that six of

His Majesty's greatest scholars were sent to teach me their language.

In about three weeks, I made progress in learning their language. The emperor frequently visited and assisted in teaching me. On one occasion, I expressed my desire for freedom.

"My lord," I began, "I would like these chains removed so I can be free."

"I see," the emperor said, placing his hand on his chin. He thought for a while. "But how can I be sure you will remain peaceful in our kingdom of Lilliput once the chains are gone?" he asked.

I raised my right hand. "I swear to it," I said solemnly. I was happy to know the name of this tiny place.

The emperor nodded. "So be it," he said, "but first you must be searched for weapons. If you have any, their enormous size could destroy us. They will be returned to you when you leave our kingdom." He turned his horse and rode away.

That afternoon, two officers arrived to make their search. They stood at my feet scratching their heads. "We are here on the emperor's orders to search you," one said. "Have you any weapons on you?" the other asked.

"See for yourself," I said. I carefully picked them up and placed them gently into each of my pockets, a pocket at a time. They squirmed around like squirrels looking for hidden nuts. If I hadn't known they were fully grown men, I would have swatted a pocket to make them stop. After they emerged from my pockets, they listed what they found. I didn't show them my secret pocket because it contained items I didn't want them to find.

When they finished, I set them down. "What will you report you found?" I asked.

"We don't know," the first officer said.

"Read your list and I will tell you," I said.

The officer, looking much relieved, unfolded his list and began to read. "A piece of cloth as large as a palace rug."

"That is my handkerchief," I said.

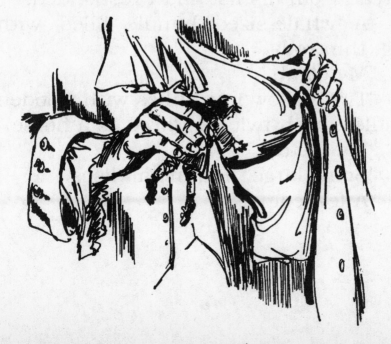

"Many sheets of thin white material covered with black figures as big as our hats," the officer said.

"That is my notebook. The black marks are writing," I said. Item by item, he read from his list and I responded.

"A whale-sized handle filled with long, thin rods."

"My comb."

"Two hollow iron tubes with wooden handles, each twice as large as a horse."

"My pistols."

"Some large, flat, metal discs."

"A few coins."

"Two shiny steel plates folded into large handles as big as doors."

"One is my pocketknife, and the other is my razor."

"A giant, clanking engine with a transparent window. Inside, two large black arrows point from the center at a circle of figures."

"My pocket watch," I said with a laugh.

"A bag bigger than a fisherman's net containing several large pieces of yellow metal."

"My purse and some gold nuggets."

"A leather pouch with pockets. One contains large metal balls of great weight. The other is filled with an unknown black powder."

"My ammunition belt with gunpowder and lead shot for my pistols."

The emperor arrived, surrounded by three thousand of his best troops. He read the officers' list. "I would like to see these things," he said to me. "Please empty your pockets and place them on the ground."

I did as I was told. But when I drew my sword from its sheath, I waved it in the air over the troops' heads. They wheeled and fell back with a loud shout.

The emperor didn't budge. "Put that down, too," he commanded, without a trace of fear in his voice.

I put the sword next to the other things. "There is one more thing I would like to show you, Your Excellency," I said. I drew my pistols and filled one with powder, but no ball. I pointed the barrel to the sky and fired. An explosion of fire and a cloud of black smoke erupted from the barrel. A hundred troops in the front rank fell to the ground as if they were struck dead. The rest ran for their lives. I glanced at the emperor. His eyes were opened wide, but he bravely stood his ground. "That is very impressive, Man Mountain," was all he said.

I piled the rest of my belongings on

the ground so the emperor could examine them. He put his hands to his ears as he walked around my watch. To him, its ticking surely sounded like musket shots. He studied each item carefully. He permitted me to keep my watch, pocketknife, razor, and other personal items. My sword, pistols, and ammunition pouch were loaded onto six large carriages and carted off. I didn't tell him my spectacles, a small telescope, and a few other things I thought might be useful were hidden in my secret pocket.

My plan was to win my freedom as soon as possible, so I did everything I

could to show that I was not a danger to the emperor or Lilliput. I practiced their language every day. I let groups of children dance on the palm of my hand or play hide-and-seek in my hair whenever they wanted. People soon lost their fear and even became friendly.

One morning as I was basking in the sun, a tiny horse and rider approached on the road leading to the city. It was a messenger sent by the emperor. "You are invited to an entertainment given in your honor by the emperor," he shouted.

I was so pleased, I answered in my normal voice, "I accept with delight." The poor man nearly fell off his horse. "I'm sorry," I quickly whispered. "Please tell

His Majesty I am honored." The man rubbed his ears and scowled at me as he rode away.

Workmen arrived that afternoon. In two days they constructed a stage the size of a small, low table in front of my house. The top was just even with my nose when I lay on my stomach the way I did when I studied ant hills as a boy.

The day of the entertainment arrived. The emperor and empress sat on thrones at one end of the table. I lay on the ground at the other. They nodded to me, and I nodded respectfully back.

"We hope you will enjoy the performance," the emperor shouted.

"I am sure I will," I replied softly.

The performers had come from all over the kingdom. There were jugglers, trick riders on horses, and acrobats, but the most impressive to me were the rope dancers.

The rope dancers strung a slender thread a foot off the ground between two poles placed two feet apart. To them the thread was as high and dangerous as a tightrope. Each dancer climbed onto the suspended thread and carefully danced to the middle. Then, all alone and with nothing to hold on to for balance, the dancer jumped high into the air. The dancers who jumped highest received the most applause from the emperor. They also received the greatest rewards. Sadly, many fell and got nothing.

I picked up one who had fallen. "Blast," he said in disgust. "I have practiced all my life to win the emperor's favor, and I failed."

I put him down and he walked off shaking his head. "Don't despair," I whispered to him, but I don't know if he was listening.

The next act was leaping and creeping. It was not as dangerous as rope dancing. The emperor enjoyed this act very much. He held out a stick in front of him, level to the ground. Each performer would then leap over the stick or creep

under it. Sometimes the emperor held the stick very high. Other times he held it very low. Each successful leaper and creeper was awarded a colorful ribbon by the emperor himself. I had seen these ribbons before and was amused that almost everyone in the royal court had one.

I applauded when the last act ended. The noise of my clapping frightened a number of horses, and many heads turned upward expecting to see thunderclouds.

"I have an act for you, Your Majesty," I said. "But first I will need time to prepare."

"We will return tomorrow," the emperor said.

I gently helped the members of the royal audience to the ground and they rode off.

I immediately went to work. With the emperor's permission, I had his woodsmen cut four tall trees from the nearby forest. They were two-feet long.

I trimmed them with my pocket knife and sharpened one end. I stuck them into the ground in a rectangular pattern so the tops were about eighteen inches in the air. I then tied the corners of my handkerchief to the poles and pulled it drum tight. I cut some smaller trees and placed them around the edges to form a guard rail so nothing could fall off.

"A perfect stage," I said when I finally finished.

The emperor and his court returned the next day. "I will put your throne in the place of honor," I said. I lifted the emperor's gilded chair into the air with him on it and placed it at one end of my aerial stage. I put the empress's throne next to his. I lifted the members of the court to the stage, but they had to be content to stand behind the emperor.

I turned my head toward the unseen side of my house. "Troops, prepare to march," I commanded. A tiny voice and the sound of a bugle answered. The emperor seemed surprised. "Ready, march," I ordered.

With a roll of drums and a chorus of trumpets, the emperor's elite guard rode into view on four-and-a-half-inch-tall steeds. They looked like a perfect collection of toy soldiers. I placed my opened hand on the ground. The first rank pranced onto my palm. I lifted the horses and riders to the stage. I did the same with the others until the whole troop was lined up in orderly rows on my handkerchief facing the emperor.

I knelt behind the audience and issued commands to the troops. "Wheel," I ordered, and they slowly turned in perfect unison. "Prepare for a mock battle," I said, and they split into two sections. They battled one another with great enthusiasm, taking care that nobody got hurt.

"Wonderful, wonderful," the emperor shouted. "Show me more."

I nodded. "The grand finale," I said

loud enough to be heard over the horizon. A cloud of dust arose and in minutes, a vast army of three thousand troops marched toward me. I rose and spread my feet wide apart. The ranks of soldiers marched through my open legs as if they were passing beneath a giant arch. The emperor crowed with delight. "A magnificent sight, Man Mountain," he shouted over the din of tiny marching feet. To me, the sound was more like the falling of light rain.

Seeing the emperor was pleased, I made my move. "Your Majesty, I have a request," I said. "I have pledged to do no harm if you will free me from these chains." I shook my leg for effect. The chains tinkled, though to the Lilliputians the sound was loud and ominous. "I ask now for my freedom."

The emperor murmured to the members of his court standing behind him. He turned to me. "All but one of my ministers have agreed to set you free," he

shouted. "They will write a document stating the conditions of your freedom."

I returned the emperor and his court to the ground, pleased that I would soon walk around Lilliput a free man. I knew that it was Skyresh Bolgolam who objected to my freedom. For some reason he chose to be my enemy.

Chapter 4

I Win My Freedom

The following day, a high-ranking minister arrived from the emperor. He unrolled a long document. "These are the rules you must abide by, Man Mountain," he said solemnly. He began to read.

"You cannot leave the country or enter the capital without permission," he cried loudly. "You must walk only on main roads and may not lie down on meadows or corn fields. When walking, you must be careful not to step on anyone, their horses, or carriages, and you may not pick up anyone without their consent. You will agree to deliver express messages for the emperor by carrying the messenger and his horse in your pocket to its destination and back."

The minister paused. "This is the most important request, so listen carefully," he warned. "You must agree to be our ally against our enemy, the Blefuscans, who live on the nearby island of Blefuscu. You must agree to do everything within your power to destroy their fleet, which is now preparing to invade Lilliput." He lifted his face to mine and in his deepest voice asked, "Do you agree, Man Mountain?"

"I agree," I answered, even though I knew the final request was written by Skyresh Bolgolam.

The minister returned to the emperor. He was back that afternoon with ten blacksmiths who removed all my chains. "I am free!" I shouted. The blacksmiths scurried for cover at the sound of my voice. "Sorry," I said, as they cautiously uncovered their ears. I turned to the minister. "My first wish is to visit your

capital city, Mildendo."

"The emperor has already granted your permission," he replied. I was overjoyed. For the first time since my capture, I was free.

I crawled into my house to get my coat. Then, with the sun on my back and the road before me, I walked to Mildendo. It was no more than twenty-three steps, but the stroll was the best of my life.

I stopped at the city wall, a two-foot-high structure that surrounded the capital. It was a foot thick with stone watchtowers every ten feet and one on each corner. I raised my coattail so it would not drag over the rooftops and stepped over the wall into the city. The people had been warned that I was coming, so the streets were empty. Even so, I walked very carefully in case there were stragglers.

A clamor of voices filled the air the moment my foot touched the cobblestone street. The rooftops, balconies, and windows were filled with people. They waved and shouted in a chorus that sounded like bees buzzing in an open hive. I waved back, but was careful to keep my voice quiet. Too many times already my voice, sneezes, or clapping had knocked Lilliputians down. I did not want to be responsible for someone falling from a roof!

"Thank you for this warm welcome," I said, bowing. My words were greeted with another shout. Children waved their hands and women waved colorful scarves.

I carefully made my way up the large central avenue. I paused to study the layout. It was like looking at a tiny toy model. The amazing difference was, Mildendo was real.

The city formed a perfect square, five hundred feet on each side. It was divided into four equal parts by two wide avenues that crossed in the center. I had no trouble walking down these avenues, but I had to avoid the smaller streets and alleys, which were only twelve inches wide. The streets were lined with three-story apartment houses and many well-stocked shops and markets. I estimated from the number of dwellings and the crowds on the rooftops that at least five hundred thousand people lived in the capital. "What a remarkable place!" I thought.

The emperor's palace stood in the center of the city, where the two wide

avenues met. It was surrounded by a two-foot-high wall. I stopped at the wall. The emperor and empress were standing in a window of the palace. "You are welcome to enter," the emperor shouted. I stepped over the wall into the palace courtyard. "I wish you could come inside so I could show you our palace," the emperor said.

I was as eager to see the palace as the emperor was to show it off. "I have an idea," I said. "Tell your servants to open all the palace windows. I will do the rest."

The emperor turned to someone behind him. In a few minutes, all the windows were opened wide.

I lay on my stomach so my head was just even with the top-story windows. The emperor and empress appeared in the window closest to my nose. The empress raised her arm and pointed around the elegant room behind her. "This is our drawing room," she said proudly. The walls were covered with fine paintings. The furniture was the most beautiful I'd ever seen. Plush drapes hung from every window.

"It is beautiful, Your Majesty," I said.

"Come," she said, "and I will show you the rest of the palace."

I proceeded to the next window, and then the next until I had looked into all of the tiny rooms. Each was as beautiful as the first. My only regret was that I could not enter.

Chapter 5

I Steal the Enemy Fleet

Two weeks after I was set free, the secretary of private affairs visited me with a message of great importance. I picked him up and put him close to my ear so he could speak in secrecy.

"The kingdoms of Lilliput and Blefuscu have been at war for many years," he confided.

"What is the cause of this war?" I asked.

"It is for a very serious matter," the secretary said solemnly. "We Lilliputians believe that the correct way to eat an egg is to break the small end first. Unfortunately, the Blefuscans think quite the opposite.

They wrongly believe it is better to break the large end first."

I held back a smile. "That is a serious matter," I said.

"Yes," the secretary replied. "We have lost many ships and many fine sailors because of it." He leaned so close to my ear that he nearly fell in. "And I fear we will lose more soon."

"What has happened?" I asked.

"The Blefuscans have gathered an

enormous fleet in their harbor," the secretary said. "They are preparing at this very moment to attack us."

I took only a moment to make my reply. "Do the Blefuscans know I am in Lilliput?" I asked.

The secretary shook his head. "No, they don't even know you exist," he said.

"Good," I answered. "Then hurry to the emperor. Tell him I will risk my life to defend Lilliput against all invaders." I put the man on his horse and he immediately galloped off to the capital.

I went at once to the coast of Lilliput. Blefuscu and Lilliput were islands separated by an eight hundred-yard-wide channel. Lilliputian sailors had told me the water was seventy glum-fluffs deep at high tide. That was about six feet. It was perfect for my plan.

I lay down behind a sand dune and withdrew my small telescope from my secret pocket. I focused it on Blefuscu. I could easily see the island and the harbor. The Blefuscans could not see me at all.

"Aha!" I exclaimed. "Just as the secretary said. The enemy fleet is anchored in a wide harbor on the opposite side of the channel." I counted each ship. There were fifty men-of-war and a flotilla of transport ships. I carefully noted the position of each one and quickly returned to my house. I called to one of my attendants. "Tell the admiral to come at once," I said. The man hurried off in a tiny puff of dust.

The admiral arrived a short time later. "I will need some supplies, Admiral," I said.

"I will get them at once," he said. "Just tell me what you need."

"I need a large supply of your strongest rope and fifty large iron bars," I said.

"They are on their way," the admiral said as he raced off on his horse. He returned with two loaded wagons. The first held many reels of rope the thickness of string. Iron bars the size of knitting needles filled the second wagon. I thanked the admiral and set to work at once.

My first task was to braid the rope into cable as thick as a child's little finger. I tested it and found it to be just right. I cut the cable into fifty equal lengths.

I twisted each iron bar into a hook and tied each hook to a length of cable. When I was done, I had fifty strong ropes with stout hooks at one end. The admiral had watched the whole process. "What are you going to do?" he asked.

"You will see," I said as I tossed the cables over my shoulder. I whistled loudly as I hurried back to the coast so that anyone on the road would hear me and get out of the way. I had no time to waste.

The tide was almost in. The channel would be at its deepest in a few minutes. I slipped off my coat, kicked off my shoes, and waded into the channel. I walked until the water was waist deep and then, with the cables firmly in my grasp, I swam toward Blefuscu. I was careful not to raise my arms out of the water. I wanted my arrival to be a surprise. I didn't stop until I reached the other side, directly in front of the enemy fleet. I stood and immediately walked toward the gathered ships.

The first enemy sailors to see me screamed in terror. Hundreds of other heads turned at the sound. They stared across the water at me as I slowly rose out of the sea. Their eyes grew large and their mouths fell open. Some shouted,

but most simply leaped into the water and swam for their lives toward the shore. I stood waist deep in water in the middle of the fleet. Every ship was empty. "The whole Blefuscan navy is mine!" I said.

I quickly attached a hook to each man-of-war. The enemy saw what I was doing, and in a few minutes a thousand tiny bowmen appeared on the shore. They fired salvo after salvo of stinging arrows at me as I worked. The arrows bounced harmlessly off my clothes, but those that hit my hands and face stung

sharply. I worried that a lucky shot would put out my eyes. "My spectacles!" I cried aloud. My eyeglasses were in my secret pocket. I stopped working and slipped them over my nose. The arrows continued to fly, but my eyes were safe. I attached the rest of the fleet to my cables in safety.

Once all of the ships were attached, I tied the cables together and threw the knotted end over my shoulder. I leaned forward and pulled, but the ships didn't budge. "What's this?" I asked. I turned to the ships. Their anchors were stuck deep in the harbor mud. I waded among the ships and cut each anchor chain with my pocketknife. The enemy soldiers and sailors watched helplessly from the shore.

When the last ship was free, I tossed the knotted cables over my shoulder again and waded out of the harbor. I walked back to Lilliput with the entire Blefuscan fleet bobbing behind me like ducks on a pond.

The emperor of Lilliput and his court were waiting for me on the shore. I was up to my shoulders in water, so all they saw was the approaching enemy ships. They were certain I had drowned. The Lilliputians braced themselves for the long-awaited attack.

I emerged from the water just as I

had done in Blefuscu. My greeting this time was loud and long. "Long live Man Mountain!" everyone cried.

I raised the tied cables, holding the captured enemy fleet over my head. "Long live the emperor of Lilliput!" I yelled. Fifty soldiers in the first rank of troops were bowled backwards by my happy shout. "You have saved my empire!" the emperor cried out. He beamed with joy. "Come, Man Mountain," he said, beckoning me with his golden sword held high in his arm.

I tied the ships to the shore so they could not drift away and walked to where the emperor and his court waited.

"Kneel," the emperor said.

I kneeled in front of the emperor's raised sword. Unfortunately, it only reached to the middle of my thigh. "May I pick you up, Your Majesty?" I asked. He nodded and I put him in the palm of my hand. I lifted him up to my face.

"In the name of His Majesty of Lilliput, me," he said gravely, "I hereby make you a Nardac of the Empire." With that, he touched the tip of my nose with his sword. I was very proud. A Nardac is Lilliput's highest honor.

Chapter 6

Charged with Treason

A few weeks later, six Blefuscan ambassadors arrived in Lilliput to sign a peace treaty. Their first request was to see me. The ambassadors were awed when I arrived at the palace. After a while, they got used to my size. One asked me to raise him up to my ear.

"I have something to tell you," he said.

I did what the ambassador requested. When he was close enough to my ear to see inside, he whispered softly into it. It sounded like a mosquito had landed on my ear. I brought my hand around to my face.

"I can't hear you unless you shout," I said. I put him back to my ear.

"This is supposed to be a secret," the ambassador screamed at the top of his lungs, "but now the whole country will hear me."

"I don't think so," I said. "The closest Lilliputians are standing at my feet."

The ambassador leaned over the edge of my hand and looked down. It was a very long way to the ground. He put his hand to his forehead to keep from fainting. When he recovered his composure, he continued. "The emperor of Blefuscu would like you to visit our country," he said.

"I will be pleased to be his guest," I answered.

Later, my enemies in Lilliput heard about the invitation and my agreement to go to Blefuscu. They said this was a sign of treason and made sure the emperor heard about it.

Not long after the Blefuscan ambassadors left, the emperor called me to the palace. "I have decided to conquer Blefuscu," he said. "Since they refuse to break their eggs at the small end the way we do, I have no other choice." The emperor then pointed at my nose. "I want you to go there at once to defeat them," he ordered.

I shook my head strongly. "No, Your Majesty," I said, "I cannot. It is against my principles to force a free and brave people into slavery."

The emperor's council heard that I had refused to defeat the Blefuscans. They supported me and the emperor's plan was put to an end. Unfortunately, our disagreement cost me his friendship. The emperor and my enemies on his council forgot the great service I had done for the country. They began to plot against me.

I was deeply saddened to lose the emperor's trust. "What can I do to heal our differences?" I wondered. Then, one night, I had my chance.

A loud knock on my door awakened me. I opened it to find a messenger from the court nervously pacing back and forth. He shouted and waved with great excitement. I put him to my ear at once, although this was one time it was almost unnecessary. "The empress's apartment is on fire!" he screamed. "You're the only one who can put it out!"

I put the man into my pocket and ran straight to the palace. I had to be extra careful not to step on anyone because the road was filled with people hurrying toward the blaze.

When I reached the palace, I could see sharp tongues of fire through the empress's open window. A shower of brightly colored sparks soared through the sky, and a thick cloud of black smoke poured from the window. Although the fire was no bigger than a biscuit burning in an oven, it was a very serious threat to the tiny palace. A hundred ladders leaned against the palace walls, and a heap of tiny buckets lay stacked in the courtyard. The buckets were smaller than sewing thimbles. The nearest source of water was a fountain across the courtyard.

Hundreds of Lilliputians formed a long bucket brigade from the fountain to the palace wall. I stood close to the window and threw each tiny bucketful of water onto the flames. The fire was too far out of control for such a trifle. "This is useless," I said. I looked around for something to beat out the flames with. I had left my coat in my house. Even the

largest carpet in the kingdom was no bigger than a lady's handkerchief. "If I don't act quickly, the palace will burn to the ground," I said. I turned to the fountain. "Get out of my way," I shouted to the line of people passing buckets. Half of them fell down in fear, and the others ran for safety.

I hopped to the fountain and kneeled down. I put my face into the water and drew until my mouth was near bursting. I raced back to the fire, waving my arms for stragglers to get out of the way. I spit a stream of water into the flames and didn't stop until the last spark died away. A shout went up from the crowd. I bowed. When I was satisfied that the fire was out, I returned to my house. I didn't bother to talk to the emperor or empress because I was sure they would be pleased.

I would learn later that spitting in the palace was against the law.

Chapter 7

I Escape to Blefuscu

Luckily, my life in Lilliput remained unchanged. I took many walks and marveled at everything I saw. The very small size of everything never ceased to amaze me. The adults were about six-inches tall and everything else was in exact proportion. An ox was between four- and five-inches tall. A goose was about the size of a sparrow. Tiny animals, like mice, were nearly invisible to me, and I never once saw a fly. The tops of the tallest trees were only seven feet tall. I could touch them easily. Small plants and vegetables were often too tiny to see.

My life was comfortable, but not always easy. I made a simple table and chair for myself from large trees that I cut in the royal park. When I needed new clothes, two hundred seamstresses sewed hundreds of strips of cloth together to make my shirts. It took three hundred tailors to make my trousers. They measured me by placing ladders against me as I kneeled on the ground. Everything I wore looked like patchwork because the widest cloth in the country was barely three inches wide.

My meals were prepared by three hundred cooks who lived in tiny houses built next to mine. Each cook was responsible for two dishes. At mealtimes, one hundred and twenty waiters carried the food and drink to my table. Twenty waiters at a time would climb onto the palm of my hand and I would put them on the table. They lifted the food up to the table on ropes slung over the side like they were drawing water from a well. The food was plentiful, but it took a lot to satisfy me. A full platter held only a mouthful and a whole barrel of drink contained only enough for a single swallow. A steak that would stuff six Lilliputians was bite-sized, and I ate turkeys and geese whole. "We have never seen anything that could eat as much as you, Man Mountain," the waiters said.

When the emperor was informed of my lifestyle, he desired to bring the royal family to dine with me.

The big day arrived. The royal family

and their court came in six elegant carriages drawn by teams of proud horses. I lifted each carriage, horses and all, onto my table. I noticed that Filmnap, the lord high treasurer, was in one. He didn't like me, and I knew at once he would use this visit to convince the emperor to banish me from the kingdom. I was right.

"Man Mountain is costing the kingdom over a million-and-a-half sprugs a day, Your Highness," Filmnap said to the

emperor. A sprug is Lilliput's most valu-
able coin. "He is also seeing the empress
in private," Filmnap added.

That was not true. The empress
enjoyed chatting with me, but she always
had a servant with her. Unfortunately,
the emperor believed Filmnap.

I heard about this when a member
of the court came to my house in secret.
I had once done him a kindness, and he
repaid it by telling me of the treachery.

"Skyresh Bolgolam, Filmnap, and others accuse you of treason," he said into my ear. "They have drawn up a list of serious charges." My secret informant pulled a scroll from his pocket and began to read: "These are the charges of treason against Man Mountain. He spit in the royal palace, which is against the law; he refused the emperor's orders to destroy Blefuscu by saying he did not believe in destroying innocent lives; he met with Blefuscu's ambassadors when they came to sue for peace; and he is planning a trip to Blefuscu."

"What will they do with me?" I asked.

My informant's face turned very dark. "The sentence for these crimes is death," he said.

I shuddered as he described how they would carry out the sentence.

"They plan to set your house on fire while you are sleeping," my informant said. "Another plan is to shoot twenty-thousand poisoned arrows into your face. Someone even suggested that your servants put poisonous juice in your clothes."

"When are they going to do this?" I asked. I knew that any of the sentences could kill me.

My informant shook his head. "Luckily, the emperor said a sentence of death was too harsh. He has ordered your life spared. Instead, they will put out your eyes."

I put my hands to my eyes. "They would do it?" I asked.

"Yes," my informant said. "Skyresh Bolgolam said that your sentence is too mild. You could still spit in the palace or take Lilliput's warships to Blefuscu. Filmnap agreed with him. He said the cost to feed you would bankrupt the treasury."

"What did the emperor say to that?" I asked. I was growing quite worried.

"He said that it would be acceptable to put out your eyes and then slowly starve you to death."

"When will they carry out this terrible sentence?" I asked. It was clear to me that I had to make plans to save my life.

"In three days," my friend said. "Twenty of His Majesty's surgeons will shoot arrows into your eyes while you lie on the ground."

"I wouldn't permit it!" I said angrily.

"They didn't think about that," my friend said. "My advice is to save yourself."

"I agree," I said. I put the man on the ground, and he slipped away.

I lay on my back in my house thinking. "I could destroy the whole country with a bombardment of boulders," I said to myself, "but I promised the emperor that I would not use my strength against him." I sat up quickly as a brilliant idea flashed through my mind. I bumped my head on the ceiling, but I ignored the pain.

"I have it!" I exclaimed. "The emperor

has given me permission to visit Blefuscu, so that's what I will do. I simply won't tell him that I'm going."

I wrapped my clothes and belongings in a bundle and crawled out of my little house for the last time. I turned toward the coast and ran there without stopping. Farmers in their houses along the way probably woke up thinking there was an earthquake.

The Lilliputian fleet lay at anchor in the harbor. I put my bundle of belongings on the largest man-of-war and cut its chain. I threw the chain over my shoulder and started toward Blefuscu. I stopped halfway across the channel and turned for a last look at the marvelous kingdom of Lilliput. Then I waded across to the royal port of Blefuscu.

Chapter 8

My Journey Home

"Man Mountain is here," shouted a lookout in the Blefuscan harbor. Soon a large crowd gathered. An escort arrived to take me to the royal court. I put him in my shirt pocket and went off to see the emperor.

"Welcome to Blefuscu," the emperor said.

"Thank you for permitting this visit," I said, bowing. I did not mention my recent problems in Lilliput.

"You are free to visit anywhere you wish," the emperor replied.

I was walking on the beach a few days after my arrival in Blefuscu when I spied a dark object bobbing in the sea. "Can it be a boat?" I exclaimed. I kicked off my shoes and ran into the water. I blinked my eyes in disbelief. "A real boat!" I shouted. "It is overturned, but from here it looks as good as new." I waded to the boat. It had been torn from a ship in a storm. Now it was mine, but I needed help to pull it ashore.

I ran to the palace to tell His Imperial Majesty. "I need twenty tall ships to help me pull the boat ashore," I said.

"You will have them at once," His Majesty replied, "and all the seamen it takes to sail them." He turned to his aide. "Tell the vice admiral of the navy to supply Man Mountain with everything he needs. Tell him to set sail at once."

I quickly returned to the beach to wait for the ships. The moment they came into view, I swam to the over-turned boat. The tiny ships circled around me as I tied cables to it. I attached the other ends to the ships. Once the floating cargo was secure, the admiral steered his fleet toward land. I worked along with the fleet and we soon had the boat beached safely on shore. An army of two thousand strong men gathered around the upside-down boat. I tied cables to one side and passed them over the top to the men. "Heave-ho!" the admiral shouted. The boat flopped upright.

"Hurrah!" I shouted. "The boat is as seaworthy as the day it was made!"

I cut two tall trees from a nearby forest and fashioned a fine set of oars. In the meantime, the emperor arrived.

"I have never seen such a giant craft," he said. "What will you do with it?"

"I will use it to return to my own country," I replied.

"I see," the emperor said. He scratched his head for a moment. "You have my permission to leave." He turned to the vice admiral. "Order your men to help Man Mountain prepare his craft for the voyage," he said.

I was grateful for the emperor's help, though he knew it would be impossible to hold me prisoner. The vice admiral's men immediately began work. Five hundred workers made sails for my boat by sewing together hundreds of strips of their strongest cloth. They made ropes and cables by twisting thirty of their thickest

ropes together. I cut down a giant tree to make a mast.

Hundreds of workers loaded my boat with everything I would need for the journey: the meat of a hundred oxen and three hundred sheep, hundreds of barrels of water, and a mountain of tiny loaves of bread. I built a small pen for six live cows, two bulls, and a small flock of sheep. I planned to take them to England to raise.

"I would like to take some of your subjects to England with me," I said to the emperor on the day the boat was ready.

The emperor shook his head violently. "Absolutely not," he said. "Search Man Mountain's pockets," he ordered. A troop of soldiers moved toward me.

"I promise I have not stolen anyone," I said.

The emperor was satisfied. "No search will be necessary," he said. Then he smiled. "I have some gifts for you to remember us by." He snapped his fingers and a carriage filled with tiny presents rolled into view. I placed the things in the palm of my hand. There were fifty small purses filled with tiny gold coins and a miniature portrait of the emperor.

"Thank you for these wondrous gifts," I said. I tucked the presents into my glove for safekeeping and stepped into my boat.

A huge crowd of Blefuscans lined the harbor to see me off. Their shouts sounded like ten thousand chirping birds. I waved and then hoisted my sail. The wind was fresh. In minutes I was out of the harbor and on my way home at last. My time in these strange lands had been a magnificent adventure.

Chapter 9

A Voyage to
Brobdingnag

For the most part, the return voyage was uneventful. I stayed in England for only two months, for my great desire to see foreign countries did not leave me. Thus, I went to the harbor to find a ship. "I am a ship's surgeon," I told the captain of the *Adventure*.

"Then you shall be my ship's surgeon," he replied. By nightfall, I was far at sea, bound for India.

We sailed for many weeks. After the *Adventure* rounded the tip of Africa, a fierce storm overtook us near the island of Madagascar.

The storm raged through the night.

By morning it was over. The sun rose over a calm sea, but we were completely lost.

"An island!" the lookout shouted, pointing at a dark shadow on the horizon.

"Prepare a boat to investigate," the captain ordered.

"I would like permission to go along," I said to the captain.

"Permission granted," he said.

The island didn't have a harbor, so we beached our small craft on the rocky shore. "I'm going to explore this place," I told the men.

I wandered a short distance up the coast. There were no signs of life anywhere, so I turned around and headed back to the boat. A terrifying scream filled the air. I raced down the beach to see what had happened.

I reached the top of a sand dune just as a giant shadow plunged everything into darkness. The boat and the *Adventure* were gone. Something had caused my crewmates to abandon me!

As suddenly as it appeared, the shadow vanished. I was alone on an unknown island, a castaway.

I staggered away from the beach, stunned by this cruel twist of fate. I stopped at the top of a steep hill and gazed inland. "What is this place?" I gasped. I could not believe my eyes. The countryside below was covered with fields of grass over twenty feet tall. Hedges as high as church steeples surrounded the fields. Treetops were hidden in the clouds. Everything was gigantic!

I stumbled down the hill to a wide road at the base of a hedge. A huge wooden stairway was built over the hedge. The steps were over six feet high! "The steps are for crossing the hedge!" I exclaimed. "But for whom?"

The ground began to shake and thunder filled the air. "An earthquake!" I screamed. I dashed into the tangled hedge for safety. The sky grew black. I was sure the earth would open up and swallow me. Then I heard voices. They were the loudest I had ever heard in my life. I peeked out of my hiding place.

Three men approached on the road. But it wasn't a road at all. It was a narrow path and the men on it were over sixty feet tall!

The men were ordinary field workers. Each one carried a scythe over his shoulder with a handle as big as a ship's mast. They covered more than thirty feet with a single step. "They're giants!" I gasped.

The leader spoke to the others in a language I had never heard. His voice boomed like cannon fire. The men nodded and climbed the steps to the field on the other side. They went to work at once, cutting what I thought were trees. I looked again. "They are cutting corn," I said in astonishment. "But the stalks are the size of full-grown trees!"

My mind raced back to Lilliput. In that strange land, I was a giant. Here, I was as small as a Lilliputian and the men in the field were the giants.

A rush of air knocked me to the ground as the sharp blade of an immense scythe passed inches over my head. "Stop!" I screamed. "I am a person down here!"

A foot as big as a cottage hovered over me, ready to crush me into the dirt like a bug. "Don't squash me!" I pleaded as loud as I could. I knew my voice was like a cricket chirp to men as big as English walnut trees. I screamed again. The foot paused and then landed gently alongside me. The blast of air knocked me on my back.

A giant hand reached down for me. The fingers opened, but then paused as if I were a tiny animal that might bite him. "I'm a man just like you," I shouted. "Well, not quite," I added. The giant grasped me by the waist between his thumb and forefinger and lifted me into the air so fast that I nearly fainted.

The giant held me in front of his face for a moment. "Put me down," I cried. I twisted and squirmed, but he was too strong. I looked into his huge eyes and put my hands together as if praying. "Please don't hurt me," I begged.

The man had no idea what I was saying, but the sound of my voice and my appearance told him that I was not a wild creature hiding in the corn like a field mouse. He put me inside his shirt pocket and hurried to his master.

The field hand put me on the ground, and the other giants gathered around me in a circle. They stared down at me as if I were a chipmunk.

"I won't try to escape," I said as loud as I could. I knew what it was like trying to hear someone as small as your finger. I dusted myself off and walked back and forth to show that I wouldn't run. The farmer spread his kerchief on the ground and nudged me onto it with his finger. He wrapped me in the kerchief and plunked me into his pocket.

After a very bumpy ride, the kerchief opened, and I found myself in the giant's house. It was huge. The farmer put me in his palm to show to his wife. "Aaaiieee!" she shrieked. The sound deafened me.

The wife backed away as if I were a spider, but her curiosity soon got the better of her. She put her nose very close to my face. I took off my hat and bowed graciously. "I am at your service, madam," I said. She smiled. I knew she would be my friend.

The farmer placed me in the center of the dining-room table, where his family was eating dinner. The table was thirty feet high, so I stayed safely in the middle near a mountain of food on an eight-foot platter.

The farmer's wife cut a tiny piece of meat into crumbs the size of turnips and handed them to me as if I were a little bird. "Thank you," I said. "I am quite hungry." I took my knife and fork from my pocket and cut the crumbs into pieces small enough for me to eat. The whole family chuckled with delight.

The farmer motioned to me to come to his end of the table. It was a long way off, so I ran. I had to dodge bread crusts as big as logs and crumbs as big as rocks. Halfway across the table, I was grabbed by a huge hand and whisked into the air. The farmer's young son, a lad of about ten, held me over his head like a toy soldier. "Put me down!" I pleaded. My heart pounded. I knew I would be killed if he dropped me. Luckily, the farmer snatched me away and put me safely on the table. He raised his hand to punish the boy.

I ran to the farmer and shouted for his attention. "Don't hurt him!" I cried. I knew I wouldn't last long in a house with a mischievous boy who had been spanked on my account. I dropped to my knees to beg for the farmer's mercy. The master understood and put his hand down. The boy returned to his chair. I knew I had made another friend.

No sooner did I turn away than a

thrumming noise filled the room. It was louder than a factory full of weaving machines. But it wasn't a machine. It was a purring black cat as big as an elephant. It sat on the farmer's wife's lap staring at me and licking her lips.

I knew if I ran, the cat would sense my fear and I would be doomed. I stood as tall as I could and drew my sword. I walked boldly to the end of the table without taking my eyes off the creature. I wagged my sword in her face. "I am not your lunch," I said firmly. The cat drew back. I replaced my sword with a flourish. I did not have to fear her anymore.

After the meal, the farmer's wife took her baby in her arms. The infant was as big as two elephants. He thought I was a toy. Reaching with his chubby hand, he grabbed me from the table and popped my head into his mouth. "Let me out of here!" I screamed. The baby spit me out, and I fell toward the floor and certain death.

The farmer's wife shouted something I did not understand and spread her apron over her lap. I plopped into it like a plum falling into a pillow. I was so weak with fear, I could not stand up. The farmer's wife carried me to a three-hundred-foot room. In it was a sixty-foot bed that was at least twenty five feet off the floor. She put me in the middle of the bed like I was a favorite doll and left the room.

No sooner did the door close then two rats the size of prize pigs entered. They smelled me and crawled onto the bed to investigate. They were big enough to devour me in a single bite.

"Go away!" I shouted. Instead, they attacked.

The first rat stood on its hind legs and lunged for my throat. I drew my sword and plunged the blade into the beast's belly. It fell dead. The second rat spun around and jumped to the floor, shrieking with fear. "I won't sleep with a dead rat on my bed, no matter how big it is," I said. I grabbed the dead rat by its six-foot tail and dragged it to the side of the bed. I gave it a kick and it fell to the floor. I was exhausted. I dropped to the bed and instantly fell asleep.

Chapter 10

My New Friend

The family's little girl was named Glumdalclitch. She was just nine years old, and she loved to play with dolls. I was put in her care, and she quickly became my best friend and protector.

Glumdalclitch was only forty-feet tall, which was small for her age. She was a very good-natured child. She gave me her doll's cradle for a bed, and she put it in the drawer of a large cabinet as protection against rats. When I pointed to something, she told me its name. In that way, I soon learned her language. "You are Grildig," she said, calling me by the name she gave me. She rarely let me out of her sight.

Soon the whole countryside knew about me. Neighbors dropped in every day to see me. "I can't believe such a tiny thing is real," one said. "Imagine," said another, "it can talk." "It does exactly what it's told," said still another.

"An attraction like this could make me a lot of money," the farmer said one day. "I will take him to the market and put him on display."

I was upset. I didn't like being treated like a curiosity, but I was helpless.

The farmer built a box to carry me in. It had a door on one side and air holes for ventilation. Glumdalclitch padded it with a quilt from her doll's bed to protect me from bruises. On market day, my master put me in the box and slung it over his saddle. Glumdalclitch climbed on her horse, and we were off. "I'll protect you," Glumdalclitch said.

The ride was worse than sailing a ship in a storm. The horse took forty-foot strides, and I bounced around inside my

box like a rag doll. By the time we arrived at the market, I was seasick.

I peeked out the window of my box. A huge man with a bell was shouting to a crowd of giants, "Hear ye, hear ye! Announcing the arrival of the tiniest man in Brobdingnag!"

My master put me in the center of a huge table. I bowed graciously to the spectators who had gathered around. "He speaks," they said as I addressed them in their own language. Glumdalclitch made certain that nobody got close enough to touch me.

I drew my sword and pretended to fight an imaginary foe. The audience shouted with glee. They happily paid for my performance. By the end of the day, I was exhausted.

My act was such a success, my master decided to take me on a tour of the entire kingdom. "I will make a fortune," he said greedily.

The next day, Glumdalclitch clutched my box safely on her lap, and we set out on horseback. "Don't worry, Grildig," she said softly. "I won't drop you."

We traveled many miles, passing giant rivers, mammoth forests, and fields the size of counties. I was the center of attention everywhere we stopped. I performed ten times a day, dancing, sword-fighting, and talking. By this time, I spoke their language well.

One day I overheard the farmer talking to himself. "I have made a fortune with my little man," he said, "but the work is killing him. He is so thin and weak, he will die soon." He scratched his chin. "I will sell him to the highest bidder."

The queen heard of me and sent word to my master that she wanted to see me. "She will be the perfect buyer," the farmer said to Glumdalclitch. "We are going to the palace."

"I am pleased to meet you, Your Highness," I said to the queen when we

were introduced. I bowed graciously and she put out a finger for me to kiss.

"You must tell me about your travels," she said.

The farmer interrupted. "He is for sale, you know, Your Majesty," he said.

"Then I shall buy him," the queen exclaimed. She gave the farmer a thousand pieces of gold bigger than carriage wheels. He eagerly accepted, and I became the property of the queen.

Glumdalclitch was very sad.

"Your Majesty!" I shouted, "I have a favor to ask."

"What is it, little man?" she said.

"I would like you to keep Glumdalclitch as my nurse," I replied.

The queen glanced at Glumdalclitch, whose frown had turned to a smile. Then the queen looked at the farmer.

"She has my permission to stay, Your Majesty," the farmer said.

"Hurrah!" I shouted. Glumdalclitch picked me up and held me next to her heart. It sounded like bass drums, but I didn't mind. I felt wonderful. When the farmer said good-bye, I felt even better.

"I must show you to His Majesty, the king," the queen said. She picked me up and swooped down a long hall, holding me high in the air. I felt like a bird.

"He's nothing but a wind-up doll," the king said when he saw me. He grabbed me from the queen's hand and put me to his ear. "But he doesn't tick," he said.

"That's because I'm a real man," I screamed into the king's ear.

He jumped. "My word," he said, "it's true. He even speaks our language." The king put me on a table. "I must have him examined by my brightest scholars," he said. "Send them at once."

Three scholars arrived within minutes. "Astounding," one said as he examined my head. "Amazing," said the second as he studied my teeth. "Incredible," said the third as he tickled my feet.

When the scholars finished studying me, they consulted with one another in a corner. "He is too small to be a dwarf," one said. "Then what is he?" asked the second. The third scholar snapped his fingers together. "I have it," he said. "The queen's little man is a trick of nature."

"Wonderful," the other scholars shouted. "That is a perfect scientific explanation."

"That's no explanation at all," I said, but the scholars didn't hear me over their smug shouts.

At last, the king was convinced I was real. He agreed to let me stay at his palace. "And your nurse may stay here, too," he said.

"She shall have a lovely apartment and a maid of her own," the queen added. "But first, Grildig needs a home, too."

The queen snapped her fingers. "Send the royal cabinetmaker," she said.

Soon, a man carrying wood and tools appeared. The queen ordered him to build a little house for me. It wasn't little at all. It was sixteen feet long and twelve feet high, with windows and a hinged roof that could be opened like a box. It had a table, a chair, a chest for my clothes, and a bed. Glumdalclitch could hold it on her lap as easily as I could hold a bird house on mine. There were metal staples on the back so it could be hooked on a servant's belt. I could sit safely inside, watching the world go by outside my windows.

"You must pad the walls," Glumdalclitch told the cabinetmaker. "He gets bumped around terribly when we ride horseback."

"I would like a lock on the door to keep rats out," I said.

When the box was finished, it was a perfect house. The chest was filled with new clothes that the queen's tailors made for me, and the table was laid with a lovely set of dishes.

The queen grew very fond of me. My table was placed next to her plate so we could dine together. She enjoyed watching me eat in miniature.

On the other hand, one bite of food for the queen could feed a dozen English farmers. She crunched lark's wings the size of turkeys, bones and all, as if they were grapes. A loaf of her bread was bigger than my house. She drank from a cup the size of a barrel.

The queen's dwarf was envious of the attention she gave me. He was only thirty feet tall. One day I said to him, "You're really a giant, you know." He thought I was teasing him.

"I'll get you for making fun of my height," he said. He grabbed me by the legs and dumped me into a silver bowl filled with cream.

"Save me!" I screamed. I swam for my life.

"Grildig!" Glumdalclitch cried. She raced across the room and pulled me from the creamer just as I was going under for the third time.

"You will be punished for that," the queen said to the dwarf.

That worried me. I did not need an angry dwarf looking for ways to get even. It didn't take him long before he tried.

The dwarf knew I hated flies. They were as big as blackbirds and flew everywhere. They swooped and soared around my head when I ate, and if I wasn't careful, they landed on my forehead.

One day the dwarf caught a handful of the biggest flies he could find and carried them to my house. He put them inside and closed the roof. Their buzzing nearly deafened me. I drew my sword. "Prepare to meet your fate, you foul flying creatures!" I shouted. Truthfully, I was uncertain if I could save myself. I slashed the air with my keen blade as they attacked like a swarm of angry birds. They fell, one by one, until the last was dead at my feet.

"My hero!" Glumdalclitch cried when she opened the roof. Word of my bravery quickly spread throughout the palace.

On another day, Glumdalclitch put my box near an open window so I could enjoy the view. I was eating a sweet cake when a swarm of giant wasps swooped into my little room. I killed four with my sword, but the others escaped. The dead wasps were as large as partridges, and their stingers were three inches long. I plucked their stingers to save as trophies. My fame as a swordsman grew.

Chapter 11

A Dangerous
Life

I enjoyed living in Brobdingnag, but there were many times when my size made life very dangerous.

One day the dwarf spied me walking under an apple tree. He was still upset with me. He shook the tree. A shower of apples as big as melons knocked me flat. I was lucky not to be killed.

Another time, the gardener's dog spotted me and snatched me up in his teeth. He carried me to his master's feet and dropped me there as if I were a rabbit. I wasn't hurt, but I shall never forget my fright.

Birds were also a nuisance. Usually, they ignored me as they hopped around looking for worms, but a hawk as large as an English pony once swooped down to carry me away. I fought him off with my sword.

One sunny day, the queen had a grand idea. "Would you like to go sailing, Grildig?" she asked.

"Oh, yes," I replied. "I miss it very much, but your smallest rowboat is bigger than a man-of-war in my country."

The queen smiled. "If you can design a boat, I will have my carpenters make it for you," she said.

I went to work at once. Soon, I had a perfect boat, complete with sails. The queen held it in her hand like a toy. "It's lovely," she said. "Aren't you eager to try it?"

I shook my head. "I would perish in a minute in the kingdom's huge rivers," I said.

"Then we shall build a river just your size," the queen said.

The queen ordered her carpenters to build a wooden trough three hundred-feet long and fifty feet wide. When it was filled with water it made a perfect lake. I rowed and sailed for hours at a time. When I was finished, Glumdalclitch hung my boat on a hook to dry.

One day, I was happily sailing on my private pond when I heard a loud "ker-chunk!" It was an immense frog, bigger than a pig. It thought my boat was a lily pad and tried to climb on. "Get off!" I screamed, beating the creature on the head with my oar until it swam away.

Of all my frights, however, the worst was because of the cook's monkey.

I was sitting near an open palace window three hundred feet above the ground enjoying the sun. I glanced out to the palace roof. The monkey, which was as large as a cow, had climbed up to my window. It snatched me in its furry paw and clambered to the roof ridge.

"Help!" I screamed. My cries were drowned by the monkey's loud chatter. Luckily, the gardener heard him. Soon a ladder appeared over the edge of the roof and the gardener saved me. He was laughing, but I was frightened out of my wits.

On another day, I heard the king playing his piano. The music was so loud that I had to sit at the far end of the room. When the king left, I decided to play it myself. The trouble was, the piano was sixty-feet long and the keys were a foot wide.

I covered the end of a long stick with mouse fur and had the piano bench placed close to the piano. I ran up and down the bench, banging the keys with my stick. The tune wasn't bad, but the running was the hardest exercise of my life.

One of my favorite pastimes was telling stories about England to the king. "In wars, we can easily blow up buildings, shoot people, and sink ships filled with men," I said.

The king was horrified. "How can anyone do such things?" he replied.

"I will be happy to show your chemists how to make gunpowder," I said.

"Never!" the king cried. "How can creatures like you, as small as insects, think of using such inhuman devices?"

I hung my head. "I have no answer to that," I said sadly.

Chapter 12

A Strange
Sea Voyage

I had been in Brobdingnag for two years when I began to feel homesick. I wanted to talk to someone without screaming at the top of my lungs. I wanted to be where I didn't have to fear being stepped on by a puppy or chased by a frog. "I would like to go home," I said to myself. "But how?"

The very next day, Glumdalclitch and I went with the king and queen to their palace near the coast. As usual, I was carried in my little house.

"I would like to visit the sea," I said to Glumdalclitch.

"I'm very tired, Grildig," she said.

"A queen's page could take me," I said.

"Well, all right," Glumdalclitch said, "but I don't like the idea at all."

The page carried my box to the seashore and placed it on a rock.

"I'm going to take a nap," I said.

The page closed the roof and wandered off to gather birds' eggs. I quickly fell asleep.

I was awakened by a terrible jolt. The rush of clapping wings filled the air as my house was whisked away. A giant sea bird carried me into the sky like a clam. It would smash my house on a rock and eat me. Suddenly, I was falling like a stone.

"Help me!" I screamed. My stomach leaped into my throat. I held tightly to my bed, fearing the worst.

My house landed in the sea with a loud splash and a solid jolt. Everything went dark. "I'm sinking!" I cried.

I glanced at the windows. They were closed tight. Not a drop of water entered.

The house stopped sinking and shot

to the surface like a cork. My little room bobbed gently on the waves like a houseboat. I peered out the window. "I am so far from land, nobody will ever find me," I moaned.

Something scraped the outside of my floating house. The house tipped sharply. It bounced over the tops of waves, dragged through the water like a fish on a string. I held on for my life.

Suddenly, it stopped. I tied a white kerchief to a stick and climbed onto a chair. I pushed open an air hole and stuck the stick into the air. "Help!" I screamed as I waved the stick back and forth.

I heard footsteps on the roof and the voices of men speaking English.

"I am an Englishman," I cried. "Please, get me out of here!"

"You are safe on our ship, mate," a voice answered. "A carpenter is coming to saw a hole for you to get out."

I was puzzled. "All you have to do is open the roof," I said. "Just put your finger through the hole and lift."

"You must be crazy, mate," the voice said. "That roof weighs a ton. I'd have to be a giant to lift it."

A hole was cut, and I climbed out

onto the deck of a sailing ship. A group of astonished sailors gathered around me. "Why, you're pygmies, just like me," I exclaimed.

"Well, if we're pygmies, we're the biggest ones in the world," the ship's captain said with a laugh.

"You are my own size!" I shouted.

That evening I described my adventures to the captain.

"I don't believe a word of it," he said.

I hurried to my house and returned with some things from my chest. "This is a wasp's stinger," I said, handing him a sharp shiny spike as long as a dagger. "And this is a man's tooth." I put a foot-long tooth on the table.

"Great heavens, it's real!" the captain exclaimed. The tooth convinced him that I was telling the truth.

We set sail for England. When I stepped off the ship, I felt like a giant. I was happy to be home, but I wondered how long it would be until I set out on another adventure.

Chapter 13

A Voyage to
Laputa

I had two more wondrous voyages before ending my travels. The first was to a strange land called Laputa.

Laputa was an island that floated through the sky. Its people had heads that were tilted sharply to one side. One eye looked up and the other looked down. Everyone was a nervous wreck because they constantly worried about the end of the world. They were afraid the earth would plunge into the sun. They were afraid it would be caught in a comet's tail. They were afraid the sun would burn out. They were so afraid, they couldn't sleep.

I told them stories of my travels, but the Laputans didn't care about the laws, governments, religions, or manners of the people I had met before. They were only interested in mathematics.

The kingdom below Laputa was called Balnibarbi. We flew there, and I was lowered to the ground on a rope. My guide was a man named Munodi.

The first people I met wore rags and were very poor. They had a wild look on their faces, and they always stared straight ahead. There wasn't a single blade of grass or ear of corn growing anywhere in Balnibarbi because the soil was so poor.

However, a short distance away, the countryside changed from barren to beautiful. Grassy meadows, green vineyards, and neat houses stretched as far as the eye could see. "These lands belong to the king," Munodi said.

"I thought so," I said.

"Would you like to see the academy?" Munodi asked. "It's where the most brilliant scientists in the kingdom work."

"That sounds interesting," I said.

The academy had many large buildings filled with people working on very odd projects. Munodi explained them to me.

"This man is extracting sunbeams from cucumbers," Munodi said. "He will store them in vials. When the weather is bad, he'll let them out."

We moved to the next laboratory, where a man was trying to build a house from the roof down. "It's the way spiders do it," the scientist said.

Outside, Munodi showed me a man herding pigs. "He has invented a new way to plough," Munodi said. "He buries thousands of acorns in a field. Then he lets the pigs loose. The field gets ploughed when the pigs dig in the dirt looking for the nuts."

"If they're looking for nuts, I can tell them where to look," I said, glancing at the academy.

"Here's a wonderful project," Munodi said. We peered into a room where a man fed colored flies to spiders. "When the spiders weave their webs, it will be colored, just like silk," the scientist said.

We visited a scientist writing on crackers.

"When people eat the crackers, they will learn what is written on them," he said proudly. "It's a wonderful way to learn."

"Here's our grandest project," Munodi said. "It's the perfect way to settle arguments. "When two people disagree, the tops of their heads are sawed off. Each top is attached to the other's head. It should end arguments forever."

"That's not all it will end," I said.

Everything I saw convinced me that this was a very strange place. I decided to return to England. I set sail a few days later and was very happy to get back home.

Chapter 14

A Voyage to
Houyhnhnm

My final voyage began a few months later. I was offered the position of captain on a ship, and I accepted.

My ship was captured by pirates. Then I was abandoned on a beach to fend for myself. I had no idea where I was.

I turned inland to search for signs of life. I soon found a well-worn path covered with horses' hoof prints. Nearby, sitting in a tree watching me, was a group of very strange-looking creatures. One jumped down from the tree and walked over to me.

"What a disagreeable-looking fellow," I said to myself. "He is disgusting."

The creature put out his hand to shake mine. I drew my sword and smacked him with its flat side. He roared in anger as the others rushed to his aid.

I was no match for the long-legged creatures. I prepared to defend my life.

Suddenly the creatures stopped. Their eyes turned white with fear. They spun on their heels and ran away. "What could have scared them so?" I wondered. I turned around. A dapple gray horse walked toward me. "It's only a horse," I said, with a sigh of relief.

The horse stopped in front of me. It bobbed its head up and down as if looking me over. When I reached out to pet him on the nose, he turned his head away as if I had offended him. He pushed my hand aside with his front hoof and neighed as if talking to himself.

Another horse joined him. They stood side by side, neighing softly to one another. "If I didn't know better, I would say they

were talking about me," I thought. "They must be magicians in disguise."

I looked the dapple gray in the eye. "If you are magicians, please help me. I am an Englishman, abandoned on your coast by pirates. May I ride on your back to safety?"

The horses shuddered. They continued talking back and forth. I heard the word "Yahoo" many times.

"Yahoo," I said.

"Houyhnhnm," the gray horse replied.

The horses led me down the path to a log building with a dirt floor. Inside was a manger filled with freshly cut hay. They nudged me into a small room.

"Great heavens!" I exclaimed. "It's filled with creatures like those I saw in the tree."

A hundred long-legged creatures sat on the floor eating raw roots. "Their limbs look just like mine," I said.

The gray horse nodded. "Yahoo," he said.

The creatures were yahoos.

The gray horse nudged me toward a pile of roots like those the yahoos were eating. "You don't expect me to eat those?" I said.

I suddenly realized the horses thought I was a yahoo. It was the shock of my life.

In a few weeks, I knew enough of the Houyhnhnm language to talk with the horses.

"We are Houyhnhnms," the gray horse said. "Tell us about yourself."

"I am an Englishman," I said. "I come from a land where yahoos rule and horses are used to pull carriages and ploughs." I told him everything I could think of. "We use war to settle arguments and make guns and bullets to do our killing. The rich have all the money and the poor have none. We have many criminals and…"

"Stop," the gray horse shouted. "I have heard enough. Your yahoos are just like ours. If I throw enough food for

fifty yahoos into a room, the stronger ones take it all and leave none for the others. You are different, but you are still a yahoo."

I refused to admit that I was a yahoo until one day a female yahoo winked at me. "It's true," I said sadly to myself. "I am a yahoo."

The gray horse became my master, and I lived in his house for three years. I made my own clothes and bread and enjoyed the Houyhnhnms' country. They lived together in peace and were very honest. They had no evil thoughts, and everything they did was governed by reason. Their main rules were friendship and kindness.

One day my master entered my room. "I have bad news," he said. "The council is upset because I let you live in my house. Either I treat you like an ordinary yahoo, or you have to go back to your country."

"I like your country," I said, "but I will leave. I'll build a boat and sail home, immediately." I set to work at once.

Soon I had a sturdy boat, stocked with food and ready to sail. My master came to the beach to wish me good luck.

"I will miss you, yahoo," he said.

"I will miss you, too," I replied. My eyes filled with tears as I launched my small craft and set sail for England.

After many days at sea, I spied an

island inhabited by European yahoos. "I would rather live with barbarians than live with yahoos," I said. I hid in a cave on an abandoned island where no one could find me. Unfortunately, a boat full of sailors came ashore one day. They found me and carried me to their ship.

"I don't want to live with yahoos," I screamed.

The sailors roared with laugher. "He is neighing just like a horse," one said.

The sailors took me aboard their ship. We docked in England a few weeks later. It was the end of my final voyage.

I have sailed all over the world, and I have seen many strange and wonderful things. This book is the true story of my travels.

Captain Lemuel Gulliver

THE END

ABOUT THE AUTHOR

Jonathan Swift was born in Dublin, Ireland, in 1667. At fifteen, he entered Trinity College but was a poor student. Once he finished school, Swift moved to London and worked as a secretary to Sir William Temple of Surrey.

In addition to poetry, Swift began writing satires on religion and government in Ireland, which brought him attention. In 1726, Swift published *Gulliver's Travels* anonymously, the only work for which he received payment. The book immediately became popular and remains so today.

Swift suffered from a disease that caused his mind to deteriorate. He founded the St. Patrick's Hospital for Imbeciles to help others like him.

In 1745, Swift died at the age of 78.

Treasury of Illustrated Classics™

Adventures of Huckleberry Finn
The Adventures of Robin Hood
The Adventures of Sherlock Holmes
The Adventures of Tom Sawyer
Alice in Wonderland
Anne of Green Gables
Black Beauty
The Call of the Wild
Gulliver's Travels
Heidi
Jane Eyre
The Legend of Sleepy Hollow
& Rip Van Winkle
A Little Princess
Little Women
Moby Dick
Oliver Twist
Peter Pan
Rebecca of Sunnybrook Farm
Robinson Crusoe
The Secret Garden
Swiss Family Robinson
Treasure Island
20,000 Leagues Under the Sea
The Wizard of Oz